Master Money the Millionaire

by ALLAN AHLBERG

02175

with pictures by
ANDRE AMSTUTZ

Puffin

Viking

PUFFIN/VIKING
Published by the Penguin Group
Penguin Books Ltd, 27 Wrights Lane, London W8 5TZ, England
Penguin Books USA Inc., 375 Hudson Street, New York, New York 10014, USA
Penguin Books Australia Ltd, Ringwood, Victoria, Australia
Penguin Books Canada Ltd, 10 Alcorn Avenue, Toronto, Ontario, Canada M4V 3B2
Penguin Books (NZ) Ltd, 182–190 Wairau Road, Auckland 10, New Zealand

Penguin Books Ltd, Registered Offices: Harmondsworth, Middlesex, England

First published by Viking 1981
7 9 10 8 6

First published in Puffin Books 1981
15 17 19 20 18 16 14

Text copyright © Allan Ahlberg, 1981
Illustrations copyright © Andre Amstutz, 1981

Educational Advisory Editor: Brian Thompson

Printed in Singapore by Imago Publishing
Set in Century Schoolbook by Filmtype Services Limited, Scarborough

ISBN Paperback 0 14 03.1246 3
ISBN Hardback 0-670-80584-X

Master Money was a lucky boy.
When he was four
he had a bucket and spade
for his birthday.
He dug a hole in the garden
and found – a box of buried treasure!
So then he had lots of money.

When he was five
he went to school.
He dug a hole in the sand-pit
and found – a bigger box
of buried treasure!
So then he had lots and lots of money.

When he was six
he went on his holidays.
He dug a hole on the beach
and found – an even bigger box
of buried treasure!
So then he had so much money,
he was a millionaire.

Master Money liked being
a millionaire.
He liked spending the money.
He liked giving it away.
He gave pocket-money to his sister.
"Thank you very much!" said his sister.
He gave pocket-money
to his mum and dad.
"Thank you very much!"
his mum and dad said.

Master Money bought:
a horse for his sister,

a car for his dad,

an aeroplane for his mum,

a bag of bones for the dog –
and a sweet shop
for himself.

BONES

At school he bought
a new black-board for his teacher.
"Just what I need!" said his teacher.
He paid a French cook
to make the dinners.
"Yum, yum!" said the children!"

He paid singing waiters to serve them.
"Tra la la!" the waiters sang.

By now Master Money was
a famous boy.
He had his picture in the newspaper.
The headline said:

Then, suddenly, when Master Money
was six and a half,
the trouble began.
Late one night Mr Creep the Crook
crept into the house,
crept up the stairs,
put Master Money in a sack –
and crept off with him!

Mr Creep took Master Money
to a secret den.
In the secret den, Mrs Creep
made a secret pot of tea
and some secret sandwiches.
Miss Creep tied Master Money
to a secret chair.
Master Creep played a secret game
of 'I Spy' with him.

The next day Master Money had his
picture in the newspaper again.
The headline said:

KIDNAPPED!
HAVE YOU SEEN THIS BOY?

The police looked everywhere
for Master Money.
His family looked everywhere too.
So did his teacher.
So did the children at school.

Then, two days later,
Mr and Mrs Money got a letter.
The letter was from Mr Creep.
It said:

I will swop you Master Money
for a MILLION POUNDS.
What do you say?
yours sincerely,
Mr Creep

P.S.
Leave the million pounds
in the secret place marked on
this map ↘

Dark Street

The Money family got the
million pounds as fast as they could.
It took every pound
that Master Money had.
Also, they had to sell the aeroplane,
the car and all the other things.
"It will be worth it," said Mrs Money.
"He is a good little lad!"

Then Mr Money left the million pounds
in the secret place.
Mr Creep crept out, crept up,
and crept off with it
Mrs Creep and the children counted it.
"It's all here, dad!"
the Creep children said.
And Master Money was set free.

The next day Master Money had his
picture in the newspaper again.
The headline said:

KIDNAPPED BOY
COMES HOME

Master Money was happy to be home.
He was not a millionaire now.
So his dad got a job,
and gave *him* pocket-money!
"Thank you very much!"
Master Money said.

Thank you very much

Three weeks later Mr Creep
and his family were caught.
But Master Money did not get
his million pounds back.

"We have not got it!"
the Creep family said.

And that was the truth.
They had spent it all.

After that nothing happened
for a while.
Then, when Master Money was seven,
he had a birthday party.
His friends from school
came to the party.
So did his teacher.

Master Money's presents were:

a football,

a football shirt,

a pair of football socks,

a pair of football boots,

a train set,

two bags of sweets –

and a bucket and spade!

Soon Master Money began digging
a hole in the garden.
Everybody gathered round.
'Perhaps something interesting
is going to happen,' they thought.
After all, Master Money was a lucky boy...